Bob and the Click of Death

1

Author: Shayne T Pattie

Editors: Charmaine Hawthorn & Peta-Jane
Pattie

Cover Illustrator: Angela Pattie

Preface

What is Morality?

Laws determine what is legal and illegal, ethics are determined by a professional group or organisation, but everyone has their own, individualised ideas of morality that has been shaped by our environment including culture, family, life experiences and geographic location.

One of the best examples of this can be found when observing or talking with people who drive motor vehicles and have had a negative driving experience caused by another person. This difference in morality and how it is expressed, can be separated into three urge responses.

Some people express this urge externally by screaming profanities, using unappealing hand signals and some go as far as to challenge complete strangers to fights.

Some people are mildly affected and have mild urges but are able to refocus by practicing calming breaths or similar.

Then there are those who have an extreme urge and wish the worst to happen to the person who has just cut them off or impacted their driving.

This is that kind of story.

Table of Contents

Bob

Bob is an average guy living in a small town called Lackyer Vale. The town has only one high school, 2 primary schools, 2 bakeries, 5 pubs and a tiny golf course, spread throughout the town. The main job opportunities in Lackyer Vale are at the meat abattoir, working farms mainly working with cattle, or picking the seasonal crops. Bob feels everyone knows everyone and as far back as he can remember, he has never felt that to be a good thing.

Bob works a very stable, but monotonous 9-5 job at the local meat abattoir. At first, he chose the abattoir job option as it seemed easy, and he wouldn't have to talk to anyone. But after several years in the same role, he has become bored, underwhelmed and now hates his job as there are no challenges or stimulation of any sort. Despite hating his job, he is too anxious to leave and start afresh, and there are not many opportunities for work or growth in his town. Bob doesn't like working with cattle as it often involves teamwork, and he felt that driving the potato harvester would mean he had to interact more with the farmers.

He lives alone in a small apartment with his pet fish called Leo Dafishy whom is his best and only friend. Bob's apartment has a minimalist feel to it. His main bedroom has a simple bed frame holding a single mattress, a plain timber cupboard with room to hang his uniform and a bench for Leo Dafishy.

His lounge room area is smaller than most people's bedrooms and holds his TV sitting on a "just big enough" bench and a one-seater lounge. His bathroom consists of a toilet, and a very small, almost tank like shower with glass walls and a glass door. His kitchen contains a small fridge, two plates, bowls, cups, cutlery and one frying pan. His small apartment is his unofficial sanctuary, where he can retreat from the world and feel safe, but some would say a minimalist or reclusive lifestyle.

Bob always had difficulty speaking with other people and found that he often said the wrong things or was ignored anyway. When he was younger, Bob had attempted to make friends during primary school, always finding it difficult, with it never working out. The awkwardness he felt after each attempt reinforced the need to avoid future attempts to socialise. Bob had no positive roles models at home growing up as his parents isolated themselves from the world and saw Bob as a nuisance, and not a child to help guide and raise.

Many times, during high school he had attempted to make friends with each time ending the same (with him being laughed at and ridiculed), leading to Bob feeling worse after each attempt. During senior high school, nearing the end of the third term, he built up the courage to attempt communication with his peers one last time. However, every time he attempted, he was overcome with anxiety and in his final attempt he spoke too quickly and stuttered leading to further teasing and verbal bullying from his peers. The outcome of this ended with him attending the school formal alone, further solidifying the belief he was better off without worrying about other people.

He attempted to interact with other people on one more occasion on his 18th birthday inviting all of his peers. However, no one arrived at his birthday party. The feelings of rejection concreted the idea of being better off alone, as he didn't need friends anyway.

As Bob grew older, being alone with his fish became a fact of life. He chose to work at the meat abattoir to earn money as it meant minimal human interaction being involved and minimal chances of being in the spotlight.

He chose a pet that did not require him leaving the house and one that was a good listener. After work most afternoons, Bob would sit and eat dinner in front of the fish tank talking to Leo Dafishy about his day. Bob occasionally wondered if Leo Dafishy's life in a small tank was also a metaphor for how he felt. Bob was not completely happy with his life, but felt there was nothing he could do to change it. Bob had always felt that if anything was to change, it would have to happen to and for him and without his direct input. What was the point in trying to improve if it never worked out, you were always ridiculed and it always led to him feeling worse anyway.

Bob and Power...

The day of Bob's change was like every other day. He finished work, smelling of stagnant blood and raw meat, and was busy thinking about what to cook for dinner.

On the way to his car after another long day at work, Bob saw a flicker of silvery light heading directly towards him. Before Bob had time to react, the silvery light hit him in the forehead. The brief event felt peculiar, but there was no pain, so Bob continued as if nothing had happened, assuming it to be the sun's glare or a trick of the brain. Bob was unaware that this very forgettable moment would impact the rest of his life in a major way, leading to his highest highs and his lowest lows.

Bob drives the same route home every day from work and is on auto pilot most days. A week after what he thought to be the sun glare or a trick of the brain, a driver cuts him off. Bob was particularly annoyed this day due to the heat of the day and his car's air-conditioning not working, and in his anger, Bob clicks his fingers and wishes the other driver dead. Bob had always believed that driving brought the worst out in people, but this belief was never directed inwardly. After clicking his fingers and having the thought, Bob continued on his way home, turned right soon after the thought and did not notice the event unfolding behind him including the other person's car losing control and crashing. This was yet again, just another day for Bob.

As Bob was unaware that the car had crashed, he had no idea that the driver of that vehicle had just died. The driver of the vehicle Janice was on her way to pick up her child from after-school care after a long day in the office. Janice was a mother of two children, with one in high school and one in primary school. Janice would normally ask the older child to look after the younger, but this particular week, Janice's older child was on school camp. This led to Janice driving faster than she normally would so she wouldn't be late picking her child up from care and led to her accidently cutting Bob off.

A week passes since Bob's first fatality resulting from his click, and Bob is at a red light with 2 cars in front of him on his way to work. A person on an electric bike appears from nowhere and instead of going to the side like Bob knew cyclists were supposed, the person decides to stop in front of the waiting cars at the lights, directly impacting Bob and triggering his immense frustration and the beginnings of road rage. He is frustrated at the rudeness of the other person and again has the thought of death and clicks his fingers.

The person then falls of their electric bike and from Bob's vantage point, the cyclist appeared to be dead.

This time, Bob becomes frozen unable to move for several seconds. Eventually he has the most obscure and weirdest thought, "what if he just caused that person's death with his thoughts". Bob quickly scoffs at the absurd thought and gets out of his car to help with calling the ambulance alongside the other 2 motorists.

Bob's second victim Fredrick was just beginning his 'Middle Aged Man In Lycra' journey, and was still learning the road rules regarding cycling. Fredrick had recently been battling with many health difficulties and felt that cycling would be a good way to become fitter, but he needed the electric motor, at least for now. Fredrick was also an avid golfer and had been organising an inter-town competition in an attempt to bring people to Lackyer Vale, which he was very passionate about.

Another month passes and another rude motorist triggers Bob's negative thought and finger click. Again, the motorist dies, and their vehicle loses control in front of Bob. This time however, Bob does not stop and help, and instead continues to drive home.

When he arrives home, he starts to consider and then believe that he might actually have the power to mortally wound a person by clicking his fingers and decides not to tell anyone including his colleagues, in fear of them thinking him mentally unwell. This triggers an internal moral struggle regarding power, death and justice.

Bob's third victim Chad was an avid gambler and was well known in the town to mistreat single women. Chad secretly hated himself and used his negative behaviours as a way to show the world how strong and masculine he was. Chad also had anger difficulties which were often expressed by fast and dangerous driving, and road rage often involving inappropriate hand gestures when he believed people were in his way, such as the one Bob witnessed before the 'Click of Death'.

After years of feeling powerless and being treated as a pushover, after all the years of people dismissing him, finally a sense of power floods through his entire body. Something in his mind snaps, and he begins to enjoy this new sensation of power, with his body feeling almost tingly, like a minor but exhilarating electric shock. He does, however, believe that he is still a good person, so he justifies his power and his behaviour by promising to only use them on motorists he believes are rude and driving recklessly, as they obviously deserve to die. He justifies this to himself further, by thinking that he would be ridding the world of these unhelpful, unstable and overall negative people, and therefore would be making the world a better place.

With less rude and negative people in the world, other people like himself would not have to experience the many negative interpersonal events that Bob himself experienced growing up. After confirming this self-justification, Bob agrees to himself that he won't use the power on people who have harmed him in the past (even if this would be improving the world) and will only focus on his future that lies ahead.

In the following 15 months Bob continues using his 'Click of Death' every time a motorist is rude, drives dangerously or vexes or inconveniences him. He justifies this last part by thinking to himself, if the motorist vexes him, then they must be a rude and negative influence on this world. Bob feels he is a fair person, and doesn't discriminate against the motorists' perceived age, ethnicity, gender or income.

He doesn't keep count at first, as he feels this might make him seem like a bad person. However, one day whilst sitting alone in his small apartment, towards the end of the 15 months, Bob estimates that he had so far killed over 26 motorists. Bob felt that he had made a positive change to the world by removing these negative people. This skewed sense of justice and morality combined with his belief there was no other possible recourse, means he doesn't lose any sleep at night over the number that is steadily increasing.

Bob never stopped to think about the families of the deceased, or the contexts of the negative people's driving as this did not fit his narrative.

Jessie the New Recruit

Many months pass and a new police recruit by the name of Jessie, starts their job in archiving and video archiving. They always wanted to join the police service and had always been good with data and statistics. Jessie was always in the top three of any of their academic subjects but found numbers especially easy and comfortable. However, Jessie also found that most people including their peers and colleagues never understood them and was often dismissed.

Jessie's childhood was not easy, and they experienced a lot of abuse and injustice. Jessie grew up in the heart of a busy city. Several gangs were well known in the city and surrounding towns and held a lot of power with various law enforcement arms. Jessie's various foster families often complained to police about the crime, to no avail. Jessie witnessed many of their foster family members being unfairly targeted by other criminals and specific police officers as a result of complaining to authorities. Jessie also received physical abuse from various foster parental figures, whom Jessie felt were only looking after them for the easily obtained government benefits. Jessie was also often targeted at school by their peers for being vaguely different and by their teachers for being an inconvenience and a "smart mouthed child". The last part Jessie felt was connected to their strength in puzzles and problem solving which often led Jessie to question and challenge their teachers when mistakes became obvious to Jessie.

As soon as Jessie turned sixteen, they left the foster system and travelled around the country. After Jessie's eighteenth birthday, they worked various "back-of-house" jobs (such as washing dishes and cleaning toilets), until they were able to join the police academy.

Whilst at the police academy, Jessie quickly became top of their class in the theory aspects but was often scolded by their trainers regarding their inability to work as a team. Thankfully though for Jessie, the state in which the academy was located was desperate for recruits, so Jessie was able to pass. To ensure they got the posting they wanted they picked the most rural town they could find on the internet.

Jessie's many negative life experiences led Jessie to want to be an honest and hardworking police officer, so that they could make a difference and help reduce the injustices they had experienced. However, Jessie also did not like large groups of people, so working in a small town was a large positive.

Jessie feels that working in this smaller town in archiving, will allow them to help society in a small way without having to directly interact with people on a regular basis. Jessie was able to meet most of their social needs through various online and often competitive puzzle games, with people from around the globe. However, because Jessie had always wanted to be a police officer to fight injustice, they never used their real name for any online interaction, instead going by the pen name 'Tardigrade'.

One day during a particularly slow workday, Jessie begins to quickly read the articles they are archiving and putting into data entry. After several hours, Jessie notices an oddly and statistically higher than accepted rate of people dying in a particular location and by a particular means.

After spending multiple weeks investigating this further, during their own time, Jessie notices that at least ninety percent of the people had died within a twenty-kilometre radius of the town hall and that they had died by natural heart failure. The roads near the town hall were poorly kept but Jessie felt that that in itself would not explain the high death rate.

Jessie starts to collect newspaper articles that would support their hypothesis and finds an alarmingly large number of articles. Jessie is concerned that their other colleagues haven't noticed this pattern, or did not care enough to notice. Jessie cuts out three examples and decides to speak with their coroner colleague.

Lackper Vale Times

Person dies from medical condition in car.

The community mourns the loss of Joe, who was driving to work when he had a sudden heart attack. Joe was a caring doctor and was much loved by many people in his town. He will be missed. He leaves behind a wife and four children.

moose numbers are expected to rise to 60,000 making China a net moose exporter for the first time. This is good news for neighbouring Mongolia, a barren moose-wasteland whose inhabitents nonetheless have an insatiable desire for the creatures. The increase in Beijing-Ulanbataar trade is anticipated to relieve pressure on the relatively strained Russian suppliers, but increase Mongolia's imbalance of trade with its larger neighbour.

Historically the only competitor to China in the far eastern moose markets has been Singapore but the

for the tenth consecuti ularly thanks to a stro the last quarter.

As moose season re researchers world wide science in an attempt year's figures. NASA scientific community t announcment of their the moon is significantl previously believed. T which is the conclus year collaborative pro profound implications community as the gra

Lackper Vale Times

Young person dies from medical condition in car.

The community mourns the loss of Nelly, who was driving to home when she had a sudden heart attack. Nelly had a promising athletics career ahead of her. She will be missed.

exporter for the first time. This is good news for neighbouring Mongolia, a barren moose-wasteland whose inhabitents nonetheless have an insatiable desire for the creatures. The increase in Beijing-Ulanbataar trade is anticipated to relieve pressure on the relatively strained Russian suppliers, but increase Mongolia's imbalance of trade with its larger neighbour.

Historically the only competitor to China in the far eastern moose

the last quarter.

As moose season re researchers world wide science in an attempt year's figures. NASA scientific community t announcment of their the moon is significantl previously believed. T which is the conclus year collaborative pro profound implications

Lackper Vale Times

Grandmother dies in passenger seat

A beloved member of the community died today in the passenger seat of her car, when her support worker had a heart attack while driving, and crashed into a tree, killing both instantly. Rachel's family has requested the community come together to celebrate Rachel's many contributions to our community. The community will miss Rachel and will hold a memorial next week

expanded moose pasture from 1.5% of arable land to nearly 3.648% and moose numbers are expected to rise to 60,000 making China a net moose exporter for the first time. This is good news for neighbouring Mongolia, a barren moose-wasteland whose inhabitents nonetheless have an insatiable desire for the creatures. The increase in Beijing-Ulanbataar trade is anticipated to relieve pressure on the relatively strained Russian suppliers, but increase Mongolia's imbalance of trade with its larger neighbour.

Historically the only competitor to China in the far eastern moose markets has been Singapore but the with numbers of Norweigian moose, known locally as elk" expected to rise for the tenth consecutive year, particularly thanks to a strong showing in the last quarter.

As moose season reaches its close, researchers world wide are turning to science in an attempt to boost next year's figures. NASA stunned the scientific community today with the announcement of their discovery that the moon is significantly smaller than previously believed. This conclusion, which is the conclusion of a ten-year collaborative project, will have profound implications for the moose community as the gravitational field

Jessie arrives at the coroner's office and double checks with their coroner colleague to confirm the information. Jessie beings the conversation with their coroner colleague:

"I have noticed an alarmingly high number of deaths within a small distance and have brought some newspaper articles as evidence".

The coroner replies "your information might be correct from a statistical perspective, but we are too busy doing real police work to notice statistical anomalies. Maybe speak with Clarence to see what he says".

After this interaction, Jessie feels embarrassed, enraged and annoyed at the same time. Jessie doesn't understand why their colleagues have such a negative behaviour towards them and why they would dismiss evidence of a potential murderer in their small town.

As a result of this very negative interaction, Jessie decides to keep this information private until they are confident enough to speak to their station manager. Jessie uses the anger that is building within to ensure they are not dismissed so easily again on the matter.

Jessie then spends several more months in their own time, investigating and watching traffic camera footage of the "accidents". Jessie eventually concludes that the only correlational pattern that existed with the deaths was a male driver in an orange mid-sized SUV. After coming to terms with this odd pattern, appreciating that there was no obvious cause, and appreciating they had no evidence, Jessie convinced themselves to speak with their station manager.

Jessie believed that the magnitude of this discovery was worth the potential social and professional challenges and tried to ignore memories of previous negative social and professional encounters in their life.

The last time Jessie had noticed that something wasn't right was during their university course, prior to applying for the police academy. Jessie noticed a pattern of overt favouritism from an older male lecturer towards a younger female student. After discussing their suspicions with other peers in their tutorial class, Jessie developed the confidence to place a complaint in.

Unfortunately, Jessie was told there was no evidence and that if they wanted to continue spreading rumours about lecturers at the university they should apply elsewhere. This interaction reinforced her already established negative beliefs about herself and other people, which made it more difficult to approach people in perceived or actual positions of power.

Armed with the newspaper articles Jessie had shown their coroner colleague, combined with snapshots and time stamps from the video footage, Jessie books a meeting with their station manager Clarence. Jessie then spends half a day convincing Clarence that this pattern is more than a correlation, that the accident rate and death rate of these strangers was extremely high (too high to be explained away by accidents), and this needed to be investigated.

Clarence reluctantly agrees there was something off about the deaths but is only able to allocate two hours a week of paid time but encourages and authorises Jessie to continue investigating in their own way and in their own time if they wanted to.

Jessie then spends the next several months focusing their investigation on the male driver of the orange SUV. During the second month of the informal investigation, Jessie noticed a pattern occurring which triggered an internal conflict. Jessie became a police officer to save lives, but if they intervened, the male driver would be aware of Jessie, and Jessie would still have no evidence to arrest the suspected perpetrator. After spending several days reconciling their conflicting emotions and thoughts about the possibility, Jessie agreed with themselves that they would have to focus on a "greater good" scenario, if they were to succeed in proving their theory and arresting the male driver.

This meant that Jessie would have to become okay with potentially letting even more people die, while they built enough evidence that they could then use to successfully charge the mystery person in order for a judge to uphold the conviction.

Jessie's investigation gave them purpose that their monotonous archiving job sometimes did not. Jessie believed that if they were to solve the (so far) unsolvable case, their colleagues would respect them, and maybe Jessie could feel in control of their own future.

Bob's Changes

At least two years had passed now for Bob since he first discovered he had a power. He continued to work at the meat abattoir, he continued to live alone with his pet fish and continued killing motorists who vexed him or impacted his driving experience.

The killing of motorists with the click of his fingers had become a normal part of his life. He no longer consciously thought about the behaviour or potential repercussions, but still subconsciously continued to only kill those whom he thought were negative people, and only while he was driving.

Bob rarely watched the news, since he didn't interact with many people from the town, and rarely spoke to his colleagues at the abattoirs. As a result, he was unaware of how his actions had impacted the town. Bob didn't know about the increased number of funerals, the slight decrease in friendliness of the town, nor did he care to notice how several smaller businesses had to close because important people had died.

The only obvious change for Bob was his presence at his workplace. He had become more confident in his work, more assertive in his communication, his work productivity improved, and he obtained a promotion. When offered further promotion, Bob chose to decline this promotion offer to shift manager because it would involve him talking to his colleagues daily.

Overall, Bob felt he was doing good by society, was feeling well and was content in how his life had turned out. Bob did not suspect for one moment that anyone would ever, could ever, find him guilty of what he called his "helping the world behaviour".

Recently however, Bob had begun to notice slight changes to the tips of his thumbs and middle fingers, as well as mild nerve pain stemming from his forehead. The tips of his thumbs and middle fingers had slowly begun to change colour, with a slight blackening of his skin and slight discolouration of the respective nails. For the last several months, Bob had assumed this to be related to his nutrition, so he had made steps to ensure he was eating a healthier diet, eating enough food and getting enough sleep.

However, Bob began to think that the discolouration might be connected to his click of death. The mild nerve pain stemming from his forehead led Bob to begin to remember the day two years ago when he was struck by the mysterious light that he had convinced himself was a trick of the brain.

For a brief moment Bob thought that his power might be coming at a cost. Bob begins to think about if the newly found power started a mutation within his body, and if so, would it affect his humanity. However, after several minutes he was able to push this thought away and continue on with his day.

Jessie's Change and Dilemma

Jessie had just spent what felt like their whole career working this case, which Jessie now referred to as "Bob's death look". Jessie had spent many hours unpaid on this case, even declining social opportunities such as work functions. Jessie was convinced that Bob was causing these deaths, but still could not find any evidence that was not correlational at best.

Jessie started to lose hope, and the police department had recently stopped paying Jessie the previously promised two hours of investigative research a week.

Feeling hopeless, powerless and disillusioned with being a police officer and the police organisation as a whole, Jessie decided that if they couldn't prove Bob was killing these people, if work would not support Jessie's investigation and if they could not stop Bob, then there had to be another way.

What if they could gently redirect Bob towards targets the law couldn't touch. Jessie was initially able to ignore any minor discomfort they felt after they had made the decision. However, they still felt a lingering, gut instinct like, feeling and subconsciously decided to further change how their viewed justice and morality. By using a "greater good" framework for morality and justice, it allowed Jessie to refocus their efforts and gave them a sense of hope again.

Jessie spent the next week focusing on their archiving job as normal, and then instead of investigating Bob, Jessie decided to make Bob an ally. Jessie used the police information to confirm Bob's address.

One night after working long hours, some of which were unpaid and focusing on their new goal, Jessie drove by Bob's house and left a mysterious letter in Bob's letter box.

In the letter Jessie had told Bob that they were aware that Bob had some type of ability to kill people from a distance and that they did not know how Bob did this, and that instead of killing people who weren't committing crimes or committing minor traffic violations, Bob could instead be using his powers for the greater good and stopping real criminals who believed themselves to be above the law.

Jessie felt that if Bob agreed, two positives would arise – innocents would stop being killed and criminals who evaded legal justice would have their punishments and justice delivered to them, albeit in a different form.

Bob's Excitement

Its Friday afternoon, Bob returns home from work smelling of stagnant blood and raw meat, checks his letter box and goes inside. He throws the mail on the bench as he normally would, but just as he was about to walk away, he notices an envelope with no window and wondered if it could be a letter, that is mixed amongst his junk mail catalogues.

Bob doesn't recognise the handwriting, and hasn't received a letter for many years, so he decides to open it and begins reading the letter. After the opening sentence, Bob drops the letter and drops to the ground, with a sudden flush of paranoia and shock. After several minutes, Bob is able to calm himself and reads the letter again.

The letter states that a person is aware of his power and behaviours. The letter also states that the person does not know how to prove it is Bob, but would like to work with Bob in managing difficult assignments. Bob decides to sleep on the information in the letter (though sleep is difficult to come by that night) and reply to the letter later.

Its Saturday morning and Bob reads the letter again and notices that the post-script has instructions on how Bob can talk to this mysterious person. Bob decides that this was worth the risk as again, "what judge, or person would believe that Bob could kill a person from a distance without any weapons".

The idea of using his power to eliminate dangerous criminals appeals to his growing sense of self-confidence and ever-changing idea of right and wrong. It also allows him to feel some excitement, as just like in his job, he had started becoming bored using his power on motorists who vexed him. This new idea of serving an even greater good then himself appealed to Bob.

Bob follows the instructions in the post-script by replying to the letter and leaves it at the requested location and continues his life as normal. Bob was unsure of any details, including who the person was that sent him the letter.

While waiting for a reply, Bob returns to his monotonous routine of working, killing motorists and talking to his fish. All the while, Bob kept hoping the reply would come soon. He wanted to know more.

Bob had continued to ignore the slight change in his fingertips and middle fingers. He did not notice or at least avoided paying attention to the slight blackening now extending further down the skin of his hand.

Jessie Picks Their Target

Two weeks later, Jessie had spent many hours investigating criminals' files in the local and state area that continued to evade justice despite multiple court attendances. Jessie had completed an exhaustive list and decided the list should be ranked.

To help Jessie pick their targets, a brief scoring system was devised. If the criminal had been caught breaking the law but was not able to be formally charged, they received five points. If the criminal committed a crime that endangered lives directly, such as assault or worse, or indirectly endangered lives such as dangerous substance sales, and they evaded justice they received twenty points. Repeat offenders received the required points, but also had extra points added, as it was obvious to Jessie that these criminals did not care about their multiple chances and "let offs".

A major trigger for Jessie was injustice, and this was evident in their scoring system.

Jessie's calculated, almost clinical research approach to creating a "target list" highlighted the moral complexity of Jessie as a person. Jessie's scoring system demonstrates their meticulous nature and their moral justification for taking lives, ranking criminals as if their fates were numbers on a chart. This system enables Jessie to maintain an emotional distance from their actions, framing each death as a necessary step toward greater justice or as Jessie thought "the greater good".

This scoring system helped Jessie prioritise whom they felt deserved to become a victim of Bob, and helped Jessie choose which targets would be easier tests for Bob's willingness and ability. Jessie felt that if Bob could remove the lower-level people, that he would eventually be ready to remove the criminal person at the top known as 'Laura'.

Jessie had always disliked injustice and had a slight fixation on people who sold dangerous substances to children, illegal substances, and sold substances to people that caused harm. Jessie was unaware that their bias might have been caused by their own childhood experiences, and like many people, felt they were capable of making rational and logical decisions based on cold calculations.

Its Wednesday and Jessie decides to assess if Bob was ready for his first task. Jessie pays a teenager on a bicycle, to deliver the letter containing the name and photo of Bob's first target. The letter contains various details to help Bob with his task, in the hope of concreting the desired outcome.

Steve

Steve is a local gang member who is well known for selling methamphetamines and other illicit substances. Steve's only life goals are to be the opposite of his father, and to make lots of money. Steve detests his father's reputation and feels like he had always been pressured to live in the shadow cast by his father.

Steve's father is the head of security for the town and is popular amongst all of the higher-ranking members of the community. As such, Steve always knew, he could use his father's influence for his own personal gain, and whenever Steve is caught by law enforcement, he is mysteriously let go within twenty-four hours.

Previously, Steve had memorised where the heaviest security camera presence around the town was and used this knowledge to influence where he sold his products.

Recently however, Steve has become more and more careless about when and how he sells his substances, as he felt untouchable because of the protection his father's position afforded him.

Despite dropping out of school at a younger age, Steve was always good with numbers which allowed him to be effective in business. He was also good at reading people and could manipulate people into doing and feeling things that benefited him. He never understood what drove people to be "good", as he felt these people were choosing to be "sheep", which he also despised.

Steve believed that he was more of an intelligent wolf, a powerful and influencing figure. Steve found that there were two main groups who were the easiest targets for his sales – teenagers and single parents. Steve had found that teenagers in his town were often struggling to find their own path in life and wanted his products to escape, while single parents were easy targets as they wanted his products because they were often tired and in need of energy, and often had lower self-image, making them easier to manipulate. Every sale reinforced Steve's already exaggerated ideas of himself.

On this particular week Steve had another great day, perhaps one of his best. He had set a personal record for selling his substances to teenagers and single parents and decides to treat himself by visiting the local pub to test his luck at the gaming tables.

Steve had always fancied himself a number "Virtuoso" and felt it was time to celebrate his sales and test his skill. Steve doesn't pay any attention to an orange SUV parked near the entrance and is excited to test his luck.

Bob's Assignment

Bob finishes his work on the Wednesday afternoon, and when he arrives home, he checks his letter box with enthusiasm. When Bob sees the letter, he runs inside and opens it. The thrill of the new challenge combined with his positive change in confidence led to Bob becoming oddly excited. Bob reads the letter, runs to his car and drives towards the local pub. Bob parks near the entrance to make his role easier.

Bob then pays great attention to the photo of his first target. Utilising internet technology, Bob is able to take a photo of the target provided in the letter and search for who the person is. Luckily for Bob, he finds several social media platforms with his targets information and is able to use this to build a solid mental picture of who his target will be. The various photos on Steve's social media platforms demonstrated strong clues about Steve's interests, fashion sense, etc.

Based on the information provided to Bob in the letter, and the information that was easily found on several social media platforms, Bob knows that he has to wait outside the gambling pub in the town. He also knows that he will be able to wait near the entrance of the pub without potential persecution, because of the nature of his power, and popularity of the town's only gambling pub.

He waits in his car, near the entrance of the pub, for what feels like half a night with windows wound up, the air conditioner on and the music gently playing. Eventually Bob notices a person that looks like the target he has in his letter, once he confirms to himself that this is the correct person, he does his 'Click of Death' and goes home.

Once home Bob attempts to sleep but finds he has too much energy from the adrenaline rush. He decides to chat with Leo Dafishy in the hope it would calm him, and this time takes notice of his finger discolouration.

Again, he thinks he might be mutating, and this might be connected with his power increasing or use of the power taking its toll on his body. But again, after several minutes he is able to distract himself.

The act of killing a person with his 'Click of Death' for an even greater cause then himself and removing bad drivers who were bad people, was very stimulating for Bob. He was eager to help the stranger who sent him the task and was eager to do what he considered to be "doing even more good for the world". It was Bob's first time killing a person who hadn't directly impacted him, but the greater good justification is all that Bob required.

Bob had been saving money for a long time without any real savings goal. Since he lived in such a small apartment with only his fish Leo Dafishy and himself as extra expenses, he had saved enough money to have a break from work if he needed to.

After a lot of thought, Bob decides to change his role at work and work part-time. Bob chats with his line manager at the abattoirs and uses the excuse of his finger discolouration, pretending to be worried about this. Bob's line manager is supportive, and Bob then accepts the demotion to his previous mundane role, so that he can focus on what he truly feels was his new life mission, a servant of "the greater good".

Assignment Complete

Thursday afternoon at work Jessie overhears two of their colleagues speaking about a local crime figure who had been found dead from a possible heart failure. Jessie's colleagues joke about how the crime figure probably used too much of his own product, and then, still discussing and joking about the death, they walk out of Jessie's ear shot.

Upon hearing this, Jessie confirms what their colleagues had been discussing and again becomes conflicted. Jessie now understands that Bob is willing to follow their instructions, and that with Bob's power they could make a difference to society, where the law could not. This provided Jessie with a sense of power that they had never experienced before.

Too many times in their life people had dismissed Jessie. Too many times in their life people had laughed at or bullied Jessie. Whilst they weren't the one directly removing bad people from society, they knew they now held the power and means to do so, and by doing so through a third party it meant they were not directly breaking the law, meaning they were still upholding justice (or at least this was Jessie's changing view of justice). Power that was far beyond anything their police role could provide, without the stress of the paperwork that often came with achieving anything meaningful.

Jessie had slowly seen their job as a financial means to an end, and they shifted their sense of justice and injustice towards utilising Bob's power.

Jessie briefly experiences a memory of when they were younger. Jessie hated seeing injustice, but they were never in a position physically or socially to stop the injustices they witnessed. Jessie remembers wanting to have the power to make real change that mattered, and this drove them to want to work in law enforcement.

Jessie then has multiple flashbacks of being ignored and overlooked in their personal and professional life.

Jessie is six years of age and notices their teaching making a math mistake. They politely raise their hand and point this out to the teacher leading to the teaching dismissing them and then later giving Jessie detention. Jessie then remembers attempting to join team sports at school and was often the last to be chosen. Jessie then begins to remember all of the faces of the people who had dismissed them and made Jessie feel tiny.

Jessie's mind is brought back to the present when Clarence walks past and knocks on Jessie's door. Clarence discusses that he has noticed that Jessie had appeared mentally absent the last few weeks. However, Jessie is able to reassure Clarence that they are okay, and as Clarence walks away Jessie then decides to focus heavily on who should be the next target for Bob and Jessie's justice.

Jessie spends several weeks picking targets, starting with lower-level criminals who kept avoiding justice, with the end goal of removing the state's crime boss who happened to have a small office in Lackyer Vale.

Jessie felt that the crime boss kept a small office in this town as they did not respect the community and knew that the town was too small for anyone to care. Jessie was able to use this thought as further motivation to make use of Bob and his power.

Without consciously deciding to, Jessie begins collecting the newspaper articles of every successful criminal that Bob removed. A scrapbook of sorts starts. The newspaper clippings reinforce Jessie's sense of justice and righteousness as they slowly slip towards a morally ambiguous belief system. The larger the 'scrapbook' becomes, the more justice and the more "good" was being done in the world.

Lackyer Va

Alleged criminal found dead

A young adult who was alleged to be connected to various substance related offences has been found dead outside a local pub. Authorities stated there was nothing unusual about the death and that he had died of natural causes. His father declined comment..

Ren
foll
imp

The
that

Lackyer Va

Alleged drug runner found d

A middle aged man was found dead today near the local high school. Medics arrived on the scene and were unable to resuscitate the man. Authorities have advised that the man was suspected to be connected to various drug related crimes in the town. Authorities report that the death is not being treated as suspicious at this time and appears to have been from natural causes.

Ren
foll
imp

The
that
rela
the

Lackyer Va

Alleged Perpetrator Released

A local teenager has reportedly been released again after it was alleged they had assaulted another person in the local library's toilet. It is alleged that this teenager is a repeat offender, and many locals are calling for harsher punishments.

Perhaps these news articles reinforced Jessie's newfound power, perhaps Jessie was changing into a person that they would not recognise in five years. For now, at least things were looking up for Jessie.

Clarence's Suspicions Arise

Clarence was the station manager and had been a police officer for over thirty years. He had spent most of his professional life in the small town and had seen many police officers come and go. Being a police officer was more than just a job for Clarence, it was his identity. As such he was a highly respected person in Lackyer Vale and was liked by many within the community. However, Clarence didn't have much of a personal life and often spent the majority of his time involved in his work.

Clarence had worked and mentored many police officers with all different interests, quirks, and personalities including many who started their career quiet, but often became more confident as they progressed in the role.

Jessie was no exception, initially Jessie was quiet and had slowly begun to warm to the role, until recently. Recently Clarence had started noticing odd behaviours from Jessie. At first Clarence was able to dismiss this, as Jessie had always been an odd person anyway. Jessie had always been quiet, noticed things other people didn't, had interests their colleagues didn't share, knew lots of random facts, knew a lot of about numbers and puzzles, was very organised and was effective at their job.

However, during the last few months, Clarence had noticed Jessie's relationship with other colleagues become even colder and distant than on previous occasions. Previously Jessie would use the societal niceties such as "good morning" and "goodbye" but recently Jessie would only smile as they passed a colleague and would often forget to say goodbye. Jessie had also started declining all social invitations from colleagues (as rare as they were) and had started working longer hours, often unpaid.

Clarence felt that Jessie might have become fixated onto the case they had previously discussed.

Clarence had also noticed Jessie locking their work draws, where previously Jessie did not. Jessie was also becoming overly protective about their workspace being theirs only, where previously Jessie would allow their colleagues to enter as needed.

Clarence's gut instinct told him there was something amiss, something that needed to be investigated. However, recently the amount of work to do, even for someone in his rank, position and enthusiasm, had increased substantially with the large number of deaths by natural causes and large number of car accidents. As a result, Clarence decided to ignore his gut instinct for now, and since Jessie was still being effective in their role, there was no need to question Jessie at this time.

Also, Clarence had made the effort on several occasions now to ask Jessie how they were going, and each time Jessie had assured Clarence they were okay. Clarence decided it was best, at least for now, to let Jessie ask for help if it was needed.

Jessie's Power...

Over the following months Jessie continued to prepare letters with targets and have them delivered to Bob. As had been the case since target one, each letter contained the target's personal address, social locations they frequented, photo, name and summary of their crime.

Jessie included the crime summaries to help continue to motivate Bob, and also to help Jessie themselves, continue to ensure their ranking system was still in effect. Each time the letter with the information would be delivered to Bob, and Bob would often have these completed within forty-eight hours.

The amount of preparation for each target, and the efficiency of Bob's work, meant Jessie was often working long hours into the night unpaid, under the guise of investigating the number of deaths.

Several times Jessie's station manager had entered the archiving office without knocking to check on Jessie's health. On each of these occasions whilst Jessie was busy preparing the targets including their files and relevant location information, Clarence had almost caught Jessie. Each time Jessie was able to successfully redirect Clarence's interest towards other work tasks and archiving responsibilities.

Subconsciously almost being caught, provided Jessie with a sense of excitement and adrenaline, which also provided extra motivation to continue their new journey of justice. Previously Jessie would never have wanted this level of power and influence. Previously Jessie had wanted to make a difference to reduce injustice in the world.

Now however, Jessie wanted to ensure justice was carried out on their terms. Now Jessie liked the adrenaline. Now

Jessie was becoming confident beyond anything they previously felt possible. Now Jessie had real power, the kind that has no consequence, the kind of power only seen in movies. Now Jessie was the one in control.

Romance for Bob?

Eventually, Bob notices that there is a connection building with whomever has been giving him the targets. Bob is unsure why, how or what this connection even means, but it was enough to spur him to think about pursuing this further. Bob had never pursued any one romantically before; he had never asked a person out, not even in primary school, had never been kissed by a friend, and most of his interactions with other people had been negative.

Bob was okay with the idea of asking this person to meet, even if it was not to have anything serious. He just wanted to understand for himself what this new feeling was, and if the other person had similar feelings. Bob also wanted to see if the other person could help him understand these new feelings.

After several days pondering this new feeling and talking to his pet Leo Dafishy, Bob decided that this new feeling must be romance and was worth pursuing. He decided he would write directly to this person, but he didn't know how to start. After writing what felt like thirty draft letters, using the internet for help, even using artificial intelligence, Bob finally had a letter he felt was good enough for the other person to see.

Bob had never had intense feelings for another person in his adulthood and was unsure what romance felt like or meant. He also had no experience writing a personal letter to anyone, especially someone he had never met.

However, due to the intensity of this new feeling, he decides to leave a letter of his own in the original drop location for the person to find. Bob does not care who the person is, what they look like, what their sexual identity is, or care about their background. Bob just wants to meet the person to see if the feeling is mutual and to see if it is worth exploring further.

Bob hopes the person is reciprocal in their response.

Romance for Jessie?

After several days, Jessie finds the letter from Bob, which was unexpected, as was the content of the letter. In the letter, Bob discusses that he has feelings for the person who he has never met, he understands that this is an odd situation to meet a person, but also wants to understand if the mystery person feels the same way.

The letter also discusses that they work great as a team, and even if there were no romantic feelings towards Bob, that Bob would still like to get to know the mystery person if possible.

Upon reading this, Jessie again has an internal conflict. Until now Bob had been a tool for justice when the legal system failed. Once Jessie had decided to use Bob's ability, they stopped seeing Bob as a person. Until now Bob had been a happy accident that also improved how Jessie had felt about themselves.

However, after reading the letter Jessie was flooded with emotions and confusion. This leads to a mini breakdown with lots of crying. After Jessie finishes crying and using two tissue boxes worth of tissues, they decide that the confusion they are feeling means that they too might have feelings for Bob.

Jessie never thought they could have feelings for a stranger, especially a killer, but they also never thought, they would be influencing people's lives, as they were currently.

Once Jessie has had time to think about the letter's request, they also then began to appreciate that without Bob and his ability, Jessie would still have no confidence, and possibly be bored of their job archiving. Jessie had heard from many movies and read in many books that if a person made you feel good about yourself and improved you in a way you felt was natural, then this person might be a good person to know.

Jessie decided to go ahead and meet with Bob eventually. However, after deciding this, Jessie became nervous for a different reason. Jessie had never dated anyone, had never been asked out, and had never had the courage to ask anyone out themselves. Jessie's plans had always involved justice and police work, living alone in an apartment with some animals. Jessie never thought they would meet anyone romantically.

Jessie decides that personal letters will be a good way to see how Bob is as a person, whilst keeping their anonymity. If the letters went well, then Jessie would be able to feel more confident about Bob, and perhaps see him as more than a tool for justice.

Letters

The next few letters with targets are accompanied by personal letters about Jessie's life, interests and other information about Jessie, without ever stating their name or occupation.

Bob continues to kill the targets and continues to reply to the personal letters about his life, events, work, his pet fish Leo Dafishy and other aspects of his life such as his social awkwardness and poor history of interacting with other people. Each time Bob would leave the reply in the original drop location.

"Dear Mystery Person,

I've never written a letter like this before. Actually, I've never written to anyone before, but I'm going to try. I always felt that I was incapable of change and incapable of connection. You've changed my life in a way I didn't think was possible. What I do for you helps to make me feel useful. It makes me feel like I'm actually doing something that matters, and that's not something I've felt before.

I don't know who you are, but I feel like I know you more than I should. Your letters, and how passionately and detailed they appear to be regarding justice not only helps me want to help but they give me purpose. I'm not sure why, but that's brought me a kind of inner peace.

Since this is my first attempt at writing a personal letter, this might feel a little much. It sounds strange, I know, but I think I'm starting to feel connected to you. Maybe even... something more.

I've never felt this way about anyone. Honestly, I don't even know what it is I'm feeling exactly, but I know it's real.

I guess I just want to know if you feel the same. I think that we currently make a good team and could continue to do so at a more personal level in the future. And if nothing else, I'd like to meet you someday, not as strangers, but as people who understand each other.

I don't care who you are or what your life is like. I just want to know you better. If you feel the same, let me know. If not, I'll still be here, doing what I do, for you, providing justice to an unjust world.

Yours, Bob"

"Dear Bob,

I didn't expect this. I didn't expect to feel anything beyond what we've been doing. I also am not good at writing personal letters and have been told I can often tell the truth too bluntly.

In the theme of honesty, until now, I had seen you as a way to bring justice in this unjust world, as a tool to stop people who felt they were above the law.

That is until I read your letter. You're right, we do make a good team, and I'm glad you feel that way. What we've done together has changed things, not just at a justice level.

I've changed as a person and felt that no one would ever understand. But hearing you talking about your experience has surprised me.

I've never thought about romance, or feelings like this. In fact, I've spent most of my life keeping people at a distance as people had often let me down and made me feel worse about myself.

However, when I read your letter, I couldn't help but wonder that maybe there's more to this than just the tasks. Maybe there is something else between us.

I don't know you the way people usually know each other, but maybe that's a good thing. Maybe it's better to connect this way, without the usual expectations, without needing to be anyone but ourselves.

I'm not sure what this is yet, or how it will end up, but I'm willing to see where it goes.

For now, I'd like to keep things like this, as letters. It feels safer for me, and for now hopefully you feel the same.

I can learn about you, and you can learn about me, without the risk of everything changing too fast.

So, tell me more about you. Your thoughts, your dreams, your life. I'll do the same.

Until then, Yours,
J"

"Dear J,

I never thought I could feel close to someone like this, especially through letters. But the more we write, the more I think about you as a person, who you are, what you're like beyond the words.

You asked about my dreams, but I've never really had any, until now. I've always lived in this small bubble, just me and my pet fish Leo Dafishy, my little apartment, and the work I do. Until recently, that work had been mundane and purposeless but safe. However, I now have purpose in life.

Now, I have noticed that I think and dream about meeting you. I think about what it would be like to sit with you and just talk. It seems we might have had similar life experiences although we decided to take different paths in response.

I guess what I'm trying to say is that I feel something for you that I don't really have the words for. It's strange and new, but it feels right, and I hope you feel it too. Even *if we never meet, I'm happy knowing we're connected like this.*

What do you dream about? What are your goals in life now, having met me?

Always,
Bob"

"Dear Bob,

I've been thinking about your question for days now. What do I dream about? It's a hard question to answer, because for so long I didn't let myself dream.

My life has been safe, controlled and orderly. I always thought that's how it had to be.

Perhaps the only dreams I have had were about justice in this unjust world.

However, now, I think I'm starting to dream again about things not to do with justice, and a lot of that has to do with you.

I dream about things I never allowed myself to want. I dream about connection, about being understood, about finally feeling like I'm not alone in the world. In a strange way, I think you've given me that already.

Through our letters, through everything we've done together, I feel less alone. I *feel like my need for justice is important but slowly becoming less important than meeting you.*

Maybe I'm dreaming of a future where we could meet, where this feeling between us could become something real. It scares me, though.

I've never been close to anyone, never let anyone in. However, with you it feels different. Safe in a good way.

I'm not ready to meet yet, but I want to keep writing. I want to keep exploring whatever this is, without losing what we already have.

Does that make sense? I hope you understand.

I feel closer to you than I ever expected, and I don't want to lose that.

Yours,
J"

"Dear J,

I understand, really. I do. I don't want to rush anything, and I don't want to make you feel pressured. The letters have become important to me, more than I ever thought they would. I feel closer to you with every word you write. I also feel that the need to use my power for Justice is slowly becoming second only to meeting you.

But I won't lie, I think about meeting you all the time now. It's become something I can't stop thinking about. I imagine what it would be like to sit across from you, to see your face, to know who you are in a way that letters can't show. But I also know that might be a lot to ask, and I don't want to push you if you're not ready. I don't care what you look like, your gender, or anything physical that might be a barrier for you.

For now, I'll keep writing. I'll keep sharing, and I'll keep waiting, if that's what you need. Just know that whenever you're ready, I'll be ready too.

I'm here. Always.

Yours,
Bob"

"Dear Bob,

I've been thinking about what you said. About meeting. It terrifies me, honestly. However, at the same time, I can't stop thinking about it either.

Maybe that's a sign.

A sign that we're both ready for something more, whatever that might be.

I've never felt this way before. Not just about you, but about anyone. I didn't think I was capable of it.

And yet, here we are, writing letters that mean more to me than I ever thought possible.

I'm not sure when I'll be ready to meet, but I think we're getting closer. I can feel it.

Until then, let's keep writing. Let's keep sharing who we are, little by little. And when the time is right, we'll know.

Until that time, I will keep sending you the tasks and will keep sending separate letters like this so we can continue to grow from a distance.

Yours,
J"

Completing Targets

Almost six months had now passed since Bob had been removing crime targets for Jessie, and Jessie felt it was time for Bob to remove the local crime boss Laura. Jessie felt that they knew a lot more about Bob as a person since the personal letters. Jessie felt that Bob would be excited for the challenge.

Jessie understands that this will be a major test for Bob, even if he does it efficiently and effectively as he had always previously.

Jessie felt that if Bob could remove Laura from this world, it would cement the idea that together Bob and Jessie would be unstoppable. It would also allow Jessie to be more comfortable in meeting Bob, knowing that Justice had been delivered.

Jessie also felt that this would free up emotional capacity for Jessie to even explore a romantic relationship with Bob if that was the direction Jessie decided to go.

Bob had enjoyed removing the targets for the mystery person 'J'. The opportunities to use his power for the greater good was his new life's purpose. The only annoying thing in Bob's life was the spreading of his skin discolouration, which he had begun to accept was a side effect of his power. For now, this side effect had no negative impact on his self-confidence. For now, the ability to kill people with his fingers from a distance overrode any potential side effects.

Laura

Laura was an average looking lady, who drove an average looking car, wore fashion trends that were often ten years out of date, and always drove themselves, with their support people sitting the back. Laura was so average looking in every physical and fiscal way possible that most people did not expect her to hold such criminal power.

Laura liked to blend in with crowds and often spent time with her female bodyguards who were also dressed to appear normal, so the group would appear to be an average group of mothers.

Law enforcements all over the state knew about her dealings, her organisation and her connections, but could never prove enough to have her held legally accountable. Laura especially enjoyed visiting Lackyer Vale because of how quiet it was, how connected she was in the town behind the scenes and how easily it was to influence outcomes outside the town using these connections. Her favourite saying was "everybody knows somebody who knows somebody" and Laura utilised this saying in a very practical sense.

Laura was soon to be visiting the local town of Bob and Jessie's, to help expand some of her businesses which required some face-to-face meetings with local figures both criminal and political. The recent death of the lower level, but efficient seller of her products, Steve, meant that it was time for Laura to become more invested into the small town of Lackyer Vale.

As always Laura arrived at the meeting in the local town hall through the front entrance, and her visitors arrived via the back entrance. The meeting was going well, and after several hours Laura stepped outside for a phone call. Whilst outside, Laura could see the local traffic driving past, hear the local birds and smell the local bakery.

One of the cars driving past on this particular day happened to be an orange SUV.

Bob had studied his latest target with enthusiasm as Jessie's letter mentioned that this target was a powerful criminal figure. Bob wanted to make himself and his romantic interest proud. Bob hoped that if he was able to remove Laura, it would free up some time for the mystery person to meet Bob.

By now, Bob had mastered his 'Click of Death' and was now able to do this while driving at normal speed without needing to slow down or pause, so he was easily able to look at Laura, click his fingers, and then continue on his way.

While Laura was on the phone, she felt sudden pain in her chest, then fell to the ground. Fifteen minutes later, when the people in the hall were starting to become restless and agitated, the local politician ran outside to find Laura dead.

The politician initially panicked, as they didn't want to be connected with Laura officially and definitely didn't want to be blamed for any murder. They then quickly spun around and organised for everyone including themselves to leave the premises via the back and then organised for one of the lower-level criminal figures to yell for help.

One of the locals heard the yell, ran over to investigate and then quickly called the ambulance. After calling the ambulance, and seeing that they were the only person there, the local person also freaked out and ran off. By the time the ambulance arrived, Laura was found alone, dead by her phone.

It was later reported in the news that a crime figure known to many law enforcement agencies had been found dead at a small-town hall. The official medical report stated that she had died from natural causes.

Time for a Date

Jessie had just finished work and while driving home was listening to the radio. The radio news broadcast reported that a well-known crime figure had recently died from a heart attack while visiting a small-town hall. The news broadcaster then continued that there were no other details at this time, but if anyone had seen anything suspicious, could they please contact their local police station.

Upon hearing this, the idea to meet up with Bob in person became realistic. Jessie felt like they now had the time and capacity to give this a go. After six months of crime targets being killed by Bob and what Jessie called Bob's 'look of Death', and after the personal letters being sent and replied too, Jessie decides it was time to risk meeting Bob face to face.

Jessie sends only a personal letter this time to Bob stating that they are finishing work at 6pm on the coming Friday and would like to meet with Bob in person, and that if Bob agrees, they will meet at the drop location.

It is Wednesday and Bob finishes work as usual, goes home and thinks of the mystery person known only as 'J'.Bob decides to go and check his mailbox to see if 'J' had any updates, or even better, if 'J' wanted to finally meet, now that Laura had been removed and justice had prevailed.

Bob goes to the mailbox and finds the letter. He excitedly tells Leo Dafishy and agrees to himself that meeting with 'J' was going to go well and cannot focus at work the remaining two days. When Friday arrives, he finishes work early, drives home, and spends time trying to "look presentable".

Bob is nervous and excited as he had never had a date but also felt calm as he felt he knew this stranger well. Unsure how to dress, he uses the internet for ideas, watches videos on how to tie a tie and then waves goodbye to Leo Dafishy. Bob then excitedly leaves home to travel to the agreed location. He quickly catches a glimpse of his hands and the spreading discolouration but ignores this and continues in his excitement to meet 'J'.

Day of the Date

Jessie is trying to finish work early on Friday as well. Ever since Bob had removed Laura and Justice had prevailed, Jessie had been thinking about Bob more than they wanted to admit. Jessie now had capacity to worry about what they would say, how they would be seen and if they would even like Bob in person.

Jessie's station boss Clarence had noticed that Jessie was about to leave for the day, and needed to speak with Jessie about a work project that they felt would be beneficial for Jessie, utilise Jessie's skills and might even improve their mood. Clarence felt that if Jessie took this new opportunity, then they might feel more empowered and feel like part of the team. Clarence rushes over to Jessie to have the chat.

Meanwhile in Jessie's mind, they are busy thinking about the meet up, or possible date. When Clarence arrives and starts talking for way too long about random stuff that Jessie cannot focus on and doesn't really care about. After what seems to be half an hour of Clarence talking, Jessie is finally able to leave work. Clarence feels the conversation went well, even though Jessie seemed a little distracted, but he puts that down to it being a Friday, and that Jessie was probably trying to take all the new information in.

Jessie knows they don't have time to look presentable but feels that Bob is the kind of person who would understand, based on the letters they had been writing. Jessie then throws an outfit over the top of most of their uniform to cover up any police symbols and begins driving to the location.

Jessie suddenly realises that they are running late and begins speeding, "but only a little bit". Jessie is so absorbed in

their own mind and not wanting to be
too late to the agreed upon destination,
that they do not see Bob's orange SUV
pulling out and accidently cuts them off.

Consequences

Bob is excitedly driving towards the agreed upon location. He is excited to finally meet 'J' and is also oddly excited to see what 'J' looks like. Would 'J' meet Bob's mental image of them, would 'J' like Bob in person? So many questions flooded Bob's mind as he drove. Bob was approximately halfway to the location when a rude driver cut them off.

Oblivious to who had just cut them off, Bob clicks his fingers, swerves to miss the car and drives to the agreed upon location. Rude drivers no longer impacted Bob much as he was able to click his fingers and be on his way without any emotional responses.

Bob then arrives at the location excited. Slowly his excitement starts to turn to worry and then eventually anger, then sadness. Bob waits two hours before deciding that 'J' wasn't coming and decides to go home.

Feeling saddened and dejected about being stood up by 'J', Bob decides to watch the news in the hope it will take his mind off his feelings. He doesn't often watch the news, but it had always been a good distraction tool when his pet fish couldn't help.

The news person states that a local police officer known as Jessie was killed today on their way home from work, having died from an unexpected heart attack while driving. The news continues to share that Jessie had been a healthy adult and had no family history of heart disease.

Bob then feels a sinking sensation in his chest. The car felt familiar although he was unsure why.

Bob continues to listen to the news, whilst in the background of his brain he kept thinking of 'J'. Suddenly,Bob starts to realise that Jessie was most likely the person he had fallen in love with. Bob also then quickly realises that Jessie was mostly likely the person he had killed with his 'Click of Death' without thinking. Bob didn't know for sure, but felt like the information on the news, combined with what Bob had learnt about 'J' from the romantic letters, combined with 'J' not showing up to the date, all confirmed that he had just killed the one person who would have understood him.

Suddenly, the idea of consequence for his actions arises all at once. His hands begin throbbing, the mild nerve pain in his forehead is felt again, the discolouration of skin and nails becomes obvious, the idea of his mutating fingers and hands being connected to killing becomes negative for perhaps the first time.

Bob's ability to justify his actions through "the greater good" and his ability to be emotionally removed from his actions fade away. Whelmed and flooded with emotions, Bob decides something has to change.

Bob then decides he needs to stop killing people and only knows one way to do this. Bob knows that will continue to have the urge to use his ability and that no matter how much he wanted to stop, he would not be able to stop. Bob had become addicted to his ability and addicted to the power of handing out justice without recompense. For the first time since he became aware of his power, Bob felt like less of a person, which triggers all of his life's previous examples of being treated as a lesser.

Bob has no friends, doesn't speak with his family and just killed the one person who might have been a positive. Following these realisations, Bob stands up, turns his TV off at the wall, wipes his face and goes to say goodbye to his fish Leo Dafishy.

Bob then stops. He had been so internally focused the last six months, so focused on meeting the mysterious person 'J' and so focused on delivering real justice, that he had not noticed Leo Dafishy's deteriorating health.

Bob notices that Leo is almost dead. Bob then gently places Leo Dafishy into a glass jar and decides to take Leo with him. With that sorted he gets into his car with his best friend by his side.

Bob then drives thirty minutes to the local hill that almost no one travels too at night and drives over the edge, only for the back wheel of his car to catch on a low-lying tree branch, midway down the hill. Bob is left stuck in his seatbelt suspended high above the ground overlooking his town below. Bob can see a great distance and had never thought about visiting the hill to see the whole town.

Bob is unsure if he wants to scream for help or struggle and let gravity and the effects of the impact do its job. So here, Bob stays stuck physically in his car, and mentally stuck in a loop of what to do...

Jessie Discovered?

The next day, following Jessie's death from natural causes, Clarence is at work. Clarence had lost officers before and knew what he had to do. He reluctantly goes to Jessie's office and decides that he could clean the office as a way to say his own goodbyes to Jessie and move forward.

Clarence is cleaning out Jessie's desk and then calls a locksmith to unlock the bottom two drawers of Jessie's personal filing cabinet. Once unlocked Clarence begins to find lots of information not relevant to Jessie's archiving role.

Clarence begins to find all the original evidence regarding Bob's murders, as well as lots of photos of recently deceased, 'hard to reach' criminals. He then finds an odd scoring system and upon a quick investigation, finds Jessie's scoring system attached with names of criminals and their respective rank within this system.

This confirms Clarence's prior suspicions about Jessie's behaviour change, which leads to Clarence feeling disappointed in himself for not acting sooner. Clarence then packs all the files from the three draws of Jessie's desk. Clarence then notices a separate cabinet that contains a basic code lock. After trying several number combinations, Clarence in his frustration, pries the top of the cabinet open enough for it to pop open.

Once open Clarence is shocked. Clarence had always thought that they had been a good station manager, and thought they were great at reading people. Nothing prepared them for what was in the separate cabinet. Clarence regathered focus, calmed nerves and then quickly skims through the scrapbook containing copies of all the recently deceased criminals, and also begins to read the multiple drafts of personal letters from Jessie to Bob that had been hidden.

Among the personal letters Clarence not only finds that Jessie and Bob had been sharing their romantic feelings for each other, but also that Jessie had been using Bob to kill criminals according to their ranked number.

Both of these revelations temporarily become too much for Clarence as he then has a flood of emotions and becomes angered. At first the anger is directed at himself for not listening to his gut instinct, then the anger is directed at Jessie for using a criminal to kill people, and then finally he becomes angered at the thought of Bob.

Something in Clarence snaps, and the calm, and confident station manager façade finally disappears and instead a vicious side to Clarence comes to the fore. Everything is Bob's fault.

Clarence decides he will now focus on finding Bob and bringing him to justice...

The End.